How Would It Feel?

Mary Beth Goddard

Illustrated by

Anna Mycek-Wodecki

Bear Cub Books
Rochester, Vermont

Bear Cub Books
One Park Street
Rochester, Vermont 05767
www.InnerTraditions.com

Bear Cub Books is a division of Bear & Company

LIBRARY OF CONGRESS CATALOGING-IN-PUBLICATION DATA
Goddard, Mary Beth, 1962–
    How would it feel? / Mary Beth Goddard ; illustrated by Anna Mycek-Wodecki.
        p. cm.
    Summary: A rhyming, illustrated exploration of the natural world, in which the reader is invited to imagine such things as waking up inside a flower or splashing down with the rain.
    ISBN 1-59143-050-X
    [1. Imagination—Fiction. 2. Nature—Fiction. 3. Stories in rhyme.] I. Mycek-Wodecki, Anna, ill. II. Title.
    PZ8.3.G5334How 2005
    [E]—dc22
                                                            2005007022

Printed and bound in China by Regent

10   9   8   7   6   5   4   3   2   1

Text design and layout by Virginia L. Scott Bowman
This book was typeset in Life with Vivante and Centaur as the display typefaces

To Alex
and
To Natalia
and all the children within us

∞

Special thanks to Judith West, our creative
editorial consultant

How Would It Feel? was written for my son, Alex. One night before he was born, I woke up with whimsical verses on my mind. I thought it would be nice to teach my child lessons from the wonders of nature.

I sent the verses to my friend Anna Mycek-Wodecki, who in turn spent the next two years illustrating the words. In each illustration there appears a small magical boy . . . Alex. Anna painted her illustrations dedicating them to Alex and to her daughter, Natalia.

Alex was born with numerous physical problems. The early years were especially difficult. To witness his spirit and strength was inspiring.

In these images, my son—who has struggled with tubes and painful manipulations—floats beyond the physical and into a magical realm. He is one with life and beyond pain.

In the course of his ten years, Alex has made many gains in strength and overall health. And I have come to realize that *How Would It Feel?* still reflects nature's lessons—but now the teacher is Alex.

In the corners of somewhere
As it spills down the floor,
As it climbs up the walls
And slips out the door,
There's a pathway to follow
For those who know how.
A journey most wondrous,
Come with me. Come now.

How would it feel
　　To ride on the breeze,
　　Aloft in a cloud ship
　　And taller than trees?

*T*hen how would it feel
  To splash down with the rain,
  Ending up in the middle
  Of a sea fish's game?

And when the game's over
And the rain is all gone,
To travel a rainbow
From back to beyond.

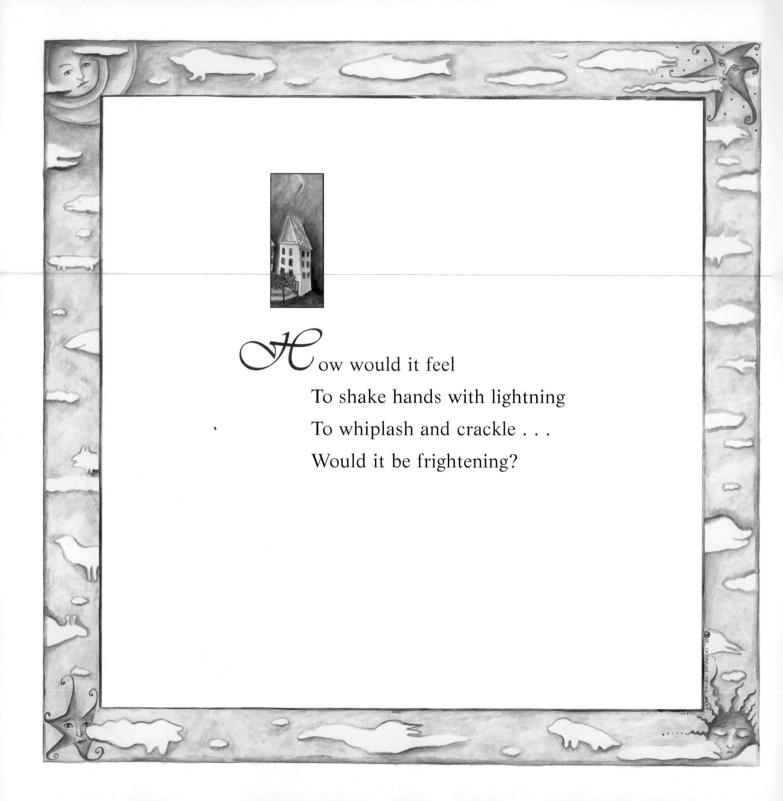

How would it feel
        To shake hands with lightning
        To whiplash and crackle . . .
        Would it be frightening?

Then when the night calms,
To see stars shooting by,
Could you swing from their arms
As they dance through the sky?

And how would you like
To wake up in a flower,
Fresh as the daffodils
After a shower?

Or how would you like
  To play tag with the sun,
  And laugh as its rays
  Try to kiss everyone?

How would it feel
If cold were a place,
Where ice had a voice
And snow had a face?

*O*r how would it feel
        To never touch land,
        Only squiggles and wiggles
        And water and sand?

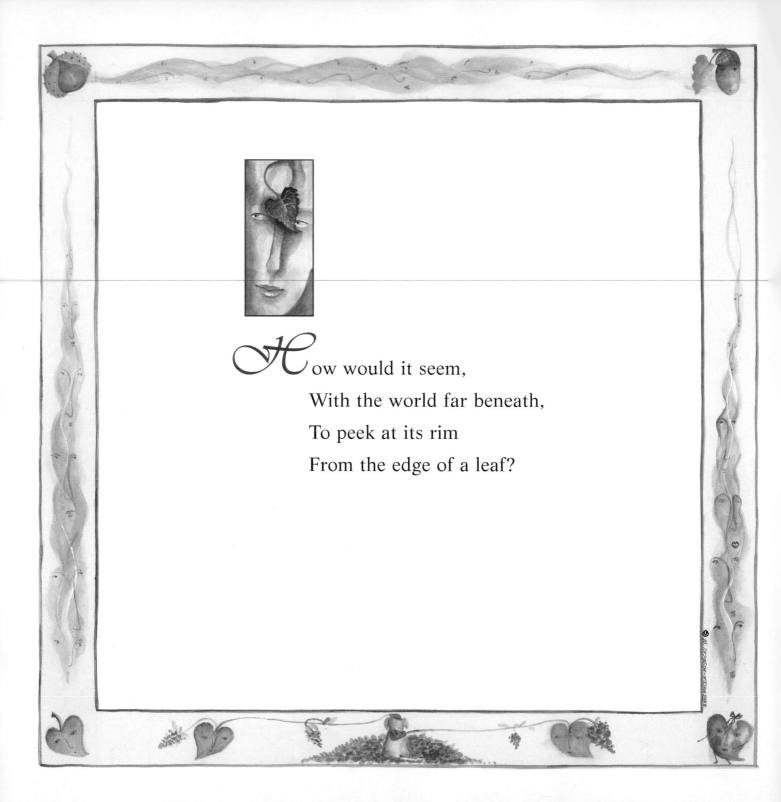

How would it seem,
With the world far beneath,
To peek at its rim
From the edge of a leaf?

*T*hen to float slowly down
 With the world coming clear,
 And to see with new eyes
 Your path reappear.

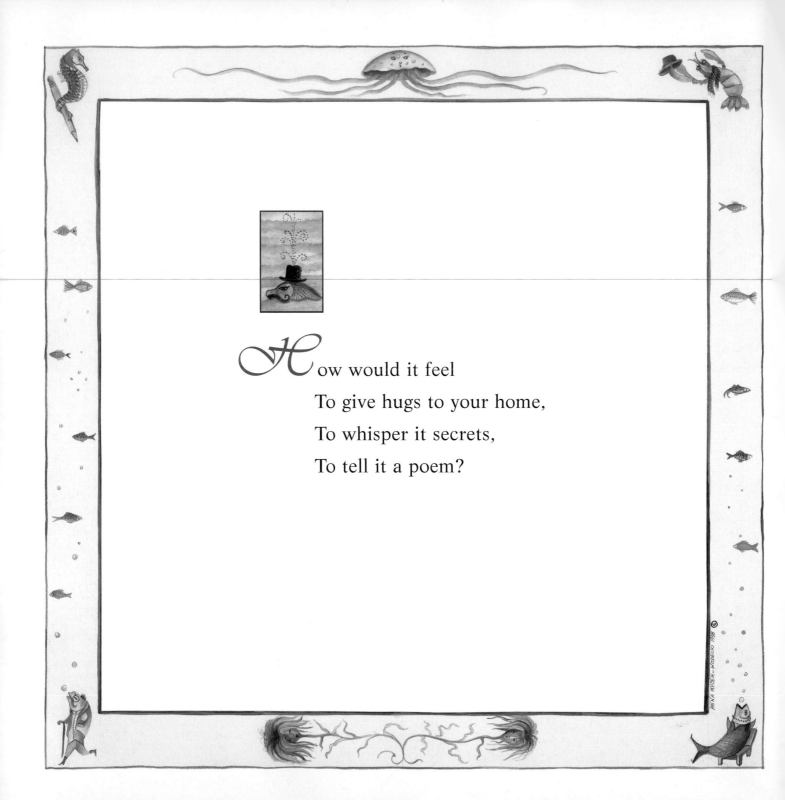

How would it feel
        To give hugs to your home,
        To whisper it secrets,
        To tell it a poem?

And how would it feel
    To be held by the moon,
    While she sings you a
    Sleepy-time, nighty-night tune?

SLEEP

SILENCE

REST

PEACE

Now it's time to go back
To your own bed and rest,
Back to the family
Who loves you the best.

DREAM

ANNA MXGEK-WOJECKI '05